THIS WALKER BOOK BELONGS TO:

_____

_____

_____

For Jack
and for Kara, fairy godmother, editor, friend
S. S.

For Cheryl, with love
P. M.

First published 2006 by Walker Books Ltd
87 Vauxhall Walk, London SE11 5HJ

This edition published 2007

2 4 6 8 10 9 7 5 3 1

Text © 2005 Sarah Sullivan
Illustrations © 2005 Paul Meisel

The right of Sarah Sullivan and Paul Meisel to be identified as
author and illustrator respectively of this work has been asserted by
them in accordance with the Copyright, Designs and Patents Act 1988

This book has been typeset in Officina Serif

Printed in China

British Library Cataloguing in Publication Data:
a catalogue record for this book
is available from the British Library

ISBN 978-1-4063-0515-9

www.walkerbooks.co.uk

DEAR BABY
Letters from Your Big Brother

Sarah Sullivan   illustrated by **Paul Meisel**

WALKER BOOKS
AND SUBSIDIARIES

LONDON • BOSTON • SYDNEY • AUCKLAND

Mum got you a rattle.

I got you a cuddly toy.

3 December

Dear Baby,

Even though you will not be born for another three weeks, I've been thinking about you a lot and wondering what life will be like after you arrive. Mum and Dad said writing you a letter might help me get ready to be a big brother.

I think I should warn you that there is not a lot of extra room in our house. Mum says there is plenty of room for a baby. I really hope she's right.

Your brother,
Mike

Shoe Box

←Your room (Ha, ha)

↖Your cot

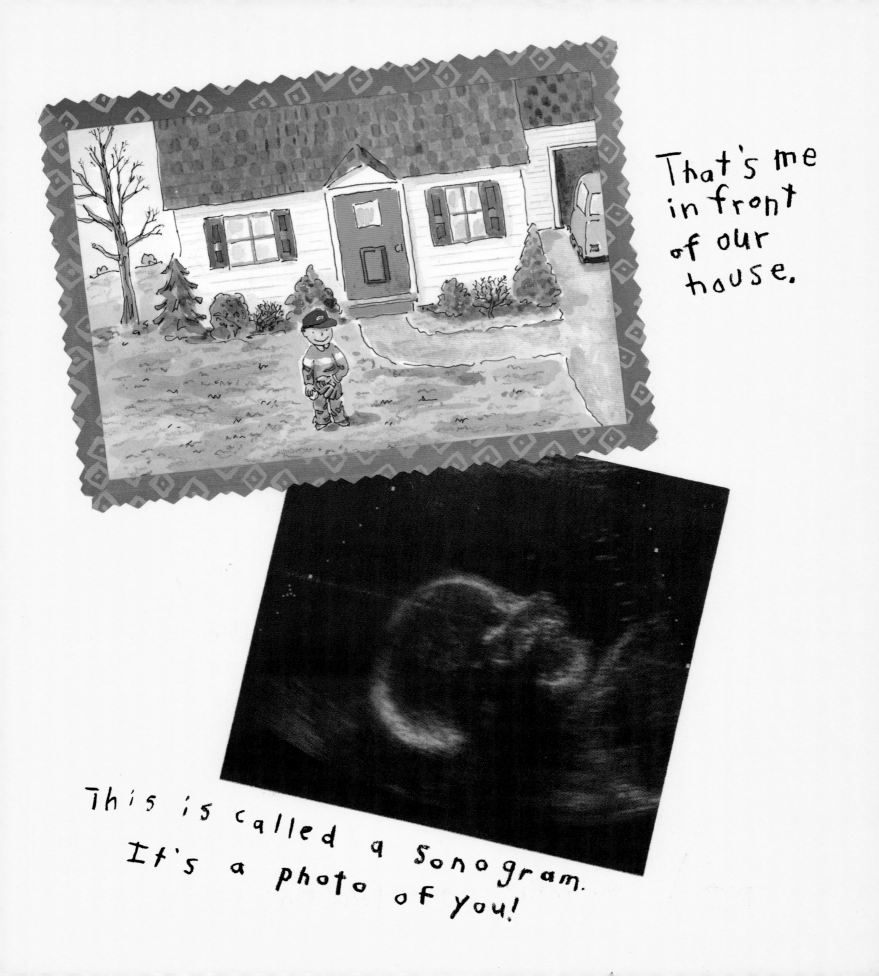

That's me in front of our house.

This is called a sonogram. It's a photo of you!

16 December

Dear Baby,

Mum and Dad said it was OK to write you another letter. I want to tell you about something that is worrying me. I haven't had a brother or sister before. I'm not sure I know how. It would be nice if you are a boy because people will give you toys that I might like to play with. Also we can play football together when you are older. Dad says girls play football too.
I hope you arrive soon (I think).

Your brother,
Mike

My favourite toy—

Powerhouse mulligan

My team—
the Rovers
Yay!

me

2 January

Dear Baby,

We are STILL waiting.
Where are you?!!!

Your brother,
Mike

You can really kick!

7 January

BABY GIRL

Dear Erica,

At last! You are born!

You came home from the hospital today. You have the tiniest hands and feet I have ever seen. And your face looks old and wrinkly. Mum and Dad think you are beautiful, but they also think asparagus tastes nice, so you can't always believe them.

Your brother (finally!),
Mike

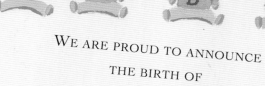

WE ARE PROUD TO ANNOUNCE

THE BIRTH OF

Erica Louise

Born 5 January

7 lbs 6 oz

49cm

We posted this
to everyone
we know.

14 February

Dear Erica,

   Mum and Dad said it would be OK for me to keep writing letters because one day you might like to read them.
   You are not so old and wrinkly-looking any more. Now you look more like yourself, which is pretty sweet, even if you do smell bad when you have a dirty nappy.

your smelly nappy

Your brother,
Mike

20 February

Dear Erica,

   Guess what? My friend Rishi is going to have a baby brother or sister too in about three months, so you will have someone to play with on our street.

   I'm sure Rishi will make a great brother, because he has a good friend to teach him what to do.

Your brother,
Mike

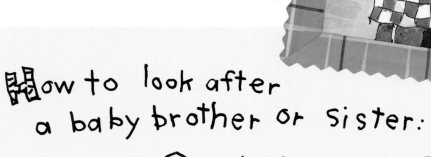

Me and Rishi

How to look after a baby brother or sister:

1. Don't eat their baby food.

Yuck.

2. Read them lots of books!

3. Make them laugh.

They like funny faces.

Grandad and Grandma think you are sooooo sweet. →

14 March

Dear Erica,

I told Rishi he can come over and practise being a big brother ANYTIME HE WANTS! I also told him he is not going to like it when the baby is born because no one will be bothered with him any more and he will be like the invisible boy at home.

He says he doesn't think it will be so bad, but you and I know better, I think. Don't we?

Your brother,
Mike

Boring
Baby ↓

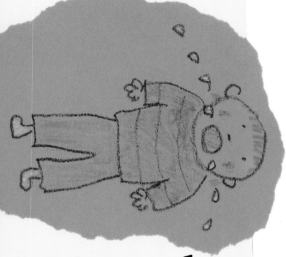

↑
Yucky
drool

14 April

Dear Erica,

I am getting fed up of everyone always wanting
to see you and hold you and talk to you all the
time. What is so amazing about a baby who just
lies there and blows spit bubbles with her mouth?
I can do much better stuff than that and nobody
notices I am here.

Your brother (who is practically invisible,
thanks to you),
Mike

I can make
better
stuff than
you.

2 May

Dear Erica,

Rishi's new baby sister arrived today. Her
name is Maya and Rishi's dad thinks she
is beautiful. Rishi says she looks like a
wrinkled-up runner bean. I told him that
is what it's like with babies. Parents always
think they are beautiful, whatever they
look like.

Your brother,
Mike

Things

chips

Maya
by
Rishi

Rishi with his
parents and Maya

that babies shouldn't eat

my hand!

Leek and potato soup

worms

toys

3 May

Dear Erica,

Rishi is going to stay at our house for a few days so his mum can rest and have plenty of energy to look after the baby. We are having pizza for dinner and Rishi says he wants to save a piece for Maya. He has a lot to learn about babies! Whoever heard of a baby eating pizza? I suppose it's up to you and me to teach him.

Your brother (who knows a lot about babies, thanks to you),
Mike

20 June

Dear Erica,

No offence, but the way you eat your food is really disgusting! Maybe you could try to keep it in your mouth for a change instead of smearing it all over the table. I am only telling you this for your own good. One day you are going to have to do it anyway.

Your brother,
Mike

Gross!

5 July

Dear Erica,

You are six months old today and Mum took you to the doctor for a check-up. I bet they gave you a jab.

I'm glad you are my sister, but I'm wondering if you could learn to take longer naps so Mum and Dad will have more time to play with me.

It's only a suggestion.

Your brother,
Mike

I thought you would never fall asleep.

Our picnic with Rishi's family

ERICA

12 August

Dear Erica,

Today I found a perfect furry worm with big, black stripes. When I took it into the house to show Mum, she screamed, **"Don't take that near the baby! She'll put it in her mouth!"** She did not think my worm was beautiful. She only thinks you are beautiful. But you are a smelly, dirty-nappy rat, if you ask me. Not beautiful like a furry worm. **Not even close!!**

Your brother,
Mike

← a Snake

a butterfly ↓

a furry worm ↘

25 August

Dear Erica,

I'm sorry I called you a dirty-nappy rat. Today was my birthday. You gave me a great present – a picture of you and me at the beach. Then you helped me blow out my candles. Now that I think about it, you're a lot better than a furry worm, and your nappies don't bother me that much.

Your brother (who is one year older today),
Mike

We had a party in the garden. →

For You, Grandson

You're Number 1!

← Grandma sent me a birthday card.

Some Things that you Will need When you go to School

Snacks →

↑ crayon

↑ money for milk ↓

6 September

Dear Erica,

   School started today. Rishi and I are in the same class. Our teacher's name is Miss Park.
   Everyone in the class had to say their name and something about their family. I said I have a little sister named Erica, who is really clever and a lot like me. Ha, ha.

Your brother,
Mike

Miss Park's class —
Can you see me?

packed lunch

pencil with rubber

a rucksack

a notebook

Look—
you
are
almost
walking!
→

27 September

Dear Erica,

I am getting a little bit cross with Rishi because he is always showing-off about his sister. He says Maya is the cleverest baby he knows. Just because she learned how to roll over does not mean she is clever. A dog can roll over. So what? You can do much more clever stuff than that! That's what I told Rishi.

Your brother,
Mike

World's Cleverest Baby

A medal I made for you

Best Baby Award

↑ Maya can only crawl!!

10 October

Dear Erica,

 Mum said I should apologize to Rishi. She says he is only being a good brother. She says I show-off about you too and Rishi doesn't get cross with me. I suppose that's true.

Your brother,
Mike

BABY OF THE YEAR

 P.S. When I apologized to Rishi, he said he was sorry too. Then I tried telling him that you are learning to walk, but first he wanted to tell me about Maya learning to crawl. Rishi's mum says that is what it's like with brothers. They always think their little sisters are the cleverest in the world.

25 October

Dear Miss Bad Baby Sister,

This is **NOT** a friendly letter. This is a business letter. This is to tell you **NOT** to play with my toys **EVER** again!! Powerhouse Mulligan has only one arm now and **NO HEAD** and we know whose fault that is, **DON'T WE?!!** You have lots of your own toys, so there is no reason to take **MINE!!**

Your brother (who is looking for a new pen pal),
Mike

DO NOT TOUCH

NO BABIES ALLOWED

you have 3 boxes of your own toys!!

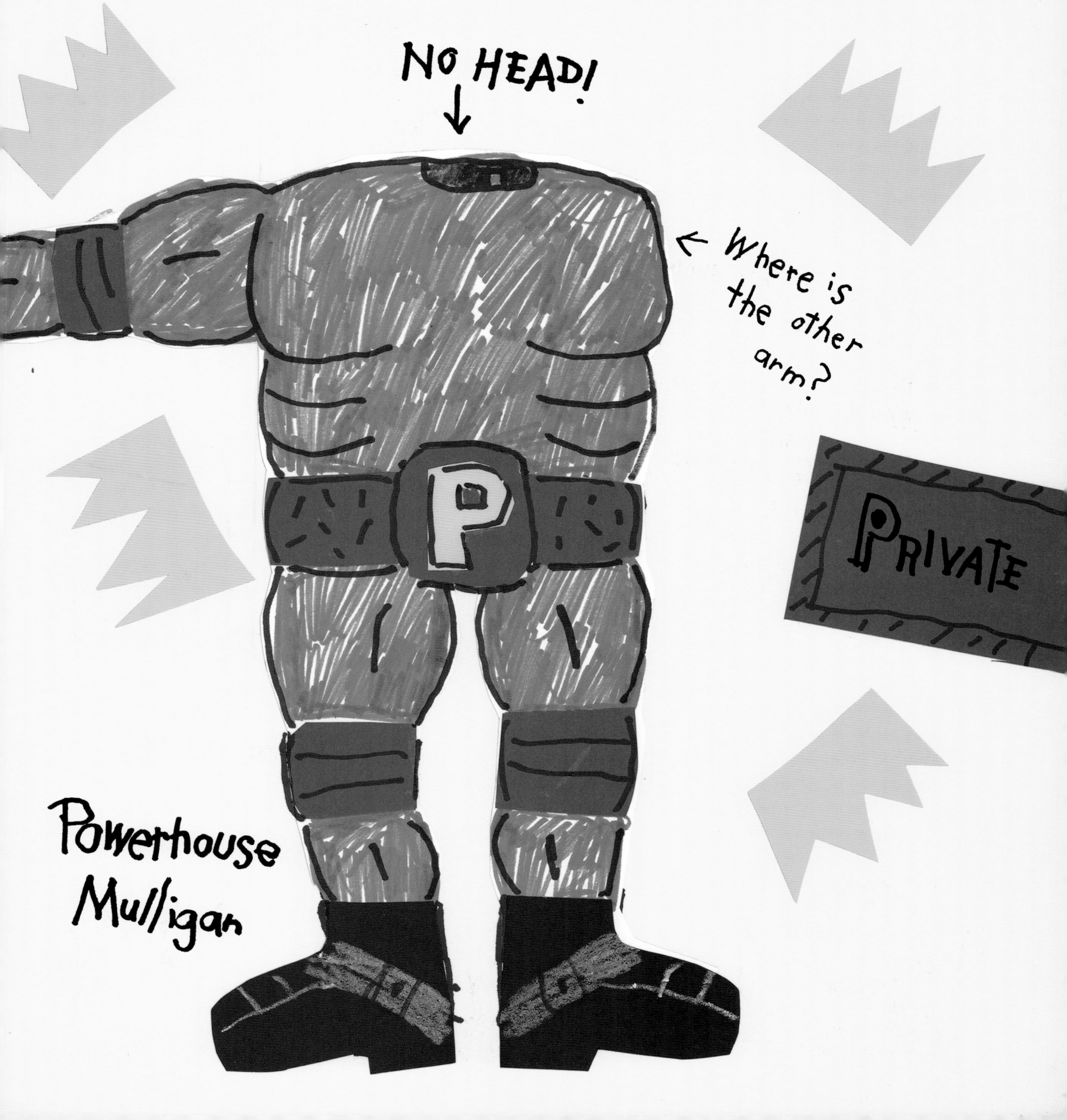
NO HEAD!
Where is the other arm?
PRIVATE
Powerhouse Mulligan

Rishi
and
Me

BOO

Maya and Erica

4 November

Dear Erica,

    You were ill today and had a temperature of 102°. Your nose was runny and your eyes looked really sad. It made me feel bad, because sometimes I wish things were like they were before you were born, when I was the only kid in the family.

    You are the best baby sister a boy could have! I hope you get well soon.

Your brother (who is sorry he ever got cross with you),
Mike

This is you when you were ill.

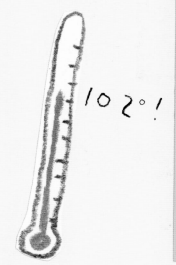

102°!

Dear Erica

Get well soon!

I made this card for you.

23 November

Dear Erica,

Today was Grandma's birthday. Grandma and Grandad came for dinner. You ate mashed potatoes with gravy, roast potato, beetroot and a slice of treacle tart. Then you smeared cranberry sauce all over Grandma's shirt. Grandma said, "Look at Erica's finger painting, Mike. She's artistic, just like you!" I have to remember to tell Rishi you're an artist too!

Your brother,
Mike

Things

↑ mashed potatoe

Grandma's Birthday! →

17 December

Dear Erica,

Today you nearly burned your hand on Mum's curling tongs till I stopped you from grabbing them. Dad says part of being a big brother is helping to stop you hurting yourself. I never knew how much Mum and Dad would depend on me. It makes me feel important. Mum says it means I am growing up. I suppose that's true.

Your brother,
Mike

If it wasn't for me, you could have fallen off your changing table!

↑you   Superbrother (me)   A monster↑

5 January

Dear Erica,

Today was your first birthday. You have changed lots since Mum and Dad brought you home. At first I wasn't sure I was going to like having you around, but now I think that having a little sister is the best thing that could have happened to me.

HAPPY BIRTHDAY, BABY SISTER!!

Your brother (who loves you a lot),
Mike

Your party
↓

WALKER BOOKS is the world's leading

independent publisher of children's books.

Working with the best authors and illustrators

we create books for all ages, from babies

to teenagers – books your child will

grow up with and always remember. So…

FOR THE BEST CHILDREN'S BOOKS,
LOOK FOR THE BEAR